"They dance so beautifully!" said the King. He was watching the twelve princesses at their lesson. "So did my wife, of course."

"Ah yes," said their teacher sadly. "The Queen was a lovely dancer. I remember her."

After the lesson, the princesses all started talking at the same time. "When can we dance at a ball?" they asked. "When can we dance with real princes?" "We never leave the palace."

"Don't ask me!" said the King. "Just stay here and be safe." He put his head in his hands and cried.

"He's still so sad about the Queen," said Annabella, the oldest princess. She sat down with him, and the others quietly left the room.

Usborne English Readers

Level 1

The Twelve Dancing Princesses

Retold by Mairi Mackinnon

Illustrated by Simona Bursi

English language consultant: Peter Viney

Contents

You can listen to the story online here:
usborne.com/twelvedancingprincessesaudio

A few days later, a servant brought the King a pair of dancing shoes. "I found these by Princess Annabella's bed," she said. "Look, they're worn out. *All* the princesses' shoes are worn out."

At breakfast, the King held up the shoes. "What happened to these? Were you *dancing* last night?

"You know we can't leave the palace," said Princess Belinda. "We just need new shoes."

That night, a servant slept outside
the princesses' bedroom and locked the
door. The next morning, she unlocked the
door… and found twelve more pairs of
worn-out shoes.

The next night, a different servant slept
there, and the night after, a different one
again. The palace shoemaker made more
new shoes every day.

"What's happening? I need to know!" said the King. He sent his servants to every town and city, and offered a reward. Soon everyone was talking about the reward. They all said different things.

"You can have half of the kingdom!" said one man.

"You can marry one of the princesses!" said another.

"Anyone can try!" said a third.

A prince heard about the reward and came to the palace. The King took him to a small bedroom, next to the princesses' room. "You must find the answer," he said. "You have three nights."

A little later, Princess Camilla knocked on the door. "We made you some hot milk," she told the prince. She smiled. She was very pretty.

"You're so kind," said the prince.
Then he sat down to wait outside
the princesses' bedroom. The
palace was quiet. The prince closed
his eyes, just for a minute…

At breakfast, the King showed him a
pair of worn-out shoes. He didn't need to
say anything.

"I'm sorry, sir," the prince said on the third morning. "I don't understand. I locked the door every night and unlocked it every morning. Nobody could go in or out."

"That's enough!" said the King. "I never want to see you again!"

More young men came to the palace. Some wanted the reward, and some just wanted to see the princesses. Every few days, another young man left the kingdom. Every morning, the palace shoemaker started making more shoes.

A soldier sat under a tree and ate some bread and cheese. An old woman sat down beside him. "Are you hungry? Would you like some?" he offered.

"Thank you, that's kind," she said. "Are you going to the palace?"

"No, why?"

The old woman told him about the reward.

"Well, I can try," said the soldier.

"Then take this magic cloak," said the old woman. "When you wear it, nobody can see you. Remember this, too: when the princesses give you hot milk, don't drink it. Good luck!"

That evening, Princess Drusilla knocked on the door and gave the soldier some hot milk. After she left, he put it outside the window. Then he sat down outside the princesses' room and waited.

Soon he heard excited voices.
He put on the cloak and carefully opened
the door. The princesses were wearing
their prettiest dresses and their new shoes.

"Why is the door open?" asked
Princess Elisa.

"It's just the wind," said Princess
Frederica. "Look, it's closed now.
Here, help me with this bed."

They pushed Princess Annabella's bed
to one side, and the soldier saw a door
in the floor. When they opened it, he
saw stairs going down. He followed the
princesses down the stairs.

"Someone touched my dress!" said
Princess Lara, the youngest.

"Don't be silly," said Princess Annabella.
"There's nobody else here. Quickly, now!"

At the bottom of the stairs, there
was a forest of silver trees. The soldier
cut off one silver branch and hid it under
his cloak.

"Did you hear that?" asked Princess Lara.

"It's nothing," said the others, "just a
bird in the trees." They walked through
the silver forest, then through a golden
one, then through a forest of jewels.

The soldier saw the lights of a palace on the other side of a lake. Twelve princes were waiting in boats. They were ready to carry the princesses across the lake. The soldier climbed into one of the boats.

"Why are we going so slowly?" asked Princess Griselda.

"I don't know," said her prince. "The boat feels strange tonight – but look, we're almost there."

Now the soldier could hear music from the palace. The ballroom doors opened and the princesses ran inside. They danced for hours, and talked and laughed with their friends. At the side of the room there were tables with food and drink. The soldier tried some. It was very good.

It was almost morning, time for the last dance. The princes and princesses went back to their boats and the soldier followed them. He ran through the three forests, then up the stairs to the princesses' bedroom. When the girls came back, he was asleep. At breakfast, he said nothing to the King.

The next night, the soldier put on his cloak and followed the princesses again. This time he cut off a golden branch, and climbed into a boat with Princess Hortensia and her prince.

He watched the dancing all night. In the morning, when the girls came back, he was asleep again.

On the third night, the soldier cut a
branch from the forest of jewels, and
climbed into Princess Irina's boat.
He tried more food and drink, and hid
a small golden cup under his cloak.

Then he climbed into Princess Jessica's
boat, ran through the forests and up the
stairs, and soon he was asleep.

"So did you find the answer?" asked the King on the third morning.

"Well, sir, look at these," said the soldier. He put the three branches and the golden cup on the table.

"But how..? He didn't… he couldn't!" said Princess Katharina.

"Your girls are very pretty and clever, and they're beautiful dancers, of course. They have some friends, and those friends also dance very well. They are nice young men – princes, too."

The King stood up angrily. The princesses were frightened, but the soldier was still telling his story.

"Come to the ball, sir," he finished. "Come and meet these princes. The princesses love dancing. They are so happy."

"Please," said Princess Lara. "Come with us tomorrow night. You need to leave the palace too, sometimes."

The King started to smile, then started to laugh. "You're just like the Queen!" he said. "I could never say no to her. Secret doors, underground forests, lakes and boats and princes... I must see this!"

About the story

Jacob and Wilhelm Grimm were brothers. They lived in Germany two hundred years ago. Together they collected and told lots of stories, like *Rapunzel, Snow White* and *The Twelve Dancing Princesses*.

The Twelve Dancing Princesses is a fairy tale – a story about magic. Fairy tales don't always have fairies in them, but they often have kings and queens, princes and princesses.

There are versions of the *Dancing Princesses* story in many European countries from Portugal to Russia. Artists love the story because of the princesses' beautiful dresses, the underground forests and lake and palace. This picture is by a Scottish artist, Anne Anderson.

Activities

The answers are on page 32.

Talk about the people in the story
Choose the right words to finish the sentences.

Princess Annabella...   The servant...   Princess Lara...

The King...   The soldier...

A.

...hears the soldier behind her in the forest.

B.

...follows the princesses to the underground forest.

C.

...finds the princesses' worn-out shoes.

D.

...sits down with the King when he is sad.

E.

...needs to know what's happening.

What happened when?

Can you put these pictures and sentences in the right order?

A.

The soldier climbed into Princess Griselda's boat.

B.

The King sent his servants to every town and city.

C.

The soldier put on the cloak and carefully opened the door.

D.

An old woman told the soldier about the reward.

E.

The princesses danced for hours.

F.

At breakfast, the King held up the shoes.

Dance, dance, dance...

One word in each sentence is wrong.
Can you choose the right word?

1.

"When can we dance with
real soldiers?"

friends   teachers   princes

2.

The town shoemaker made
more new shoes every week.

village   palace   clever

3.

The ballroom doors opened
and the princesses waited inside.

danced   ran   slept

4.

"Your girls are clever
dancers, of course."

happy   beautiful   silly

What happened next?

Choose the right sentence for each picture.

1. "We made you some hot milk," Princess Camilla told the prince.

A. The prince followed the princesses to the underground forest.

B. The prince drank the milk and fell asleep.

2. The soldier offered the old woman some bread and cheese.

A. The old woman gave him a magic cloak.

B. The old woman didn't want any.

3. "Someone touched my dress!" said Princess Lara.

A. "It was just a bird in the trees," said the others.

B. "There's nobody else here," said Princess Annabella.

What does the soldier think?

Choose the right thought for each part of the story.

A.
Why don't I take something to show the king?

B.
Hmm, I'm rather hungry.

C.
It's a strange story. I'm interested.

D.
What's happening? Where are they going?

1.

2.

3.

4.

Word list

almost (adv) when you are not yet at a place but you are very near, you are almost there.

ball (n) a grand, formal dance.

ballroom (n) a room especially for dancing.

bottom (n) the lowest part of something.

branch (n) a part of a tree. A branch usually has leaves or flowers on it.

cloak (n) a type of large coat without arms. A cloak covers most of your body.

follow (v) if you follow someone, you go behind or after them.

good luck (excl) when you want good things to happen for a person, or you want things to go well for them, you say, "Good luck!"

jewel (n) a precious stone. For example, a diamond is a jewel.

kind (adj) good and nice to other people.

kingdom (n) the country of a king or queen.

knock (v) when you knock, you make a noise with your hand on a door to tell someone you are there.

lake (n) an area of water with land all around it.

lock (v) when you close a
door with a key, you lock it.

offer (v) when you say you are going
to give something to someone or do
something for someone, you offer it.

pair (n) two of something together,
for example shoes or socks.

palace (n) the home of a king or queen.

reward (n) when you offer money for
something, especially something that is
lost or stolen, that money is a reward.

servant (n) someone who works for another
person, especially inside their home.

silver (adj) made of a shiny precious
metal (less expensive than gold).

soldier (n) someone who fights for their
country in an army and sometimes in a war.

worn out (adj) when you wear something or
use something until it looks old and broken,
and you can't use it any more, it is worn out.

Answers

Talk about the people in the story

Princess Annabella... D
The King... E
The servant... C
The soldier... B
Princess Lara... A

What happened when?

F, B, D, C, A, E

Dance, dance, dance...

1. ~~soldiers~~ princes
2. ~~town~~ palace
3. ~~waited~~ ran
4. ~~clever~~ beautiful

What happened next?

1. B
2. A
3. B

What does the soldier think?

1. C
2. D
3. B
4. A

You can find information about
other Usborne English Readers here:
usborne.com/englishreaders

Designed by Hope Reynolds
Series designer: Laura Nelson Norris
Edited by Jane Chisholm

Page 24: picture of the Brothers Grimm © Lebrecht Music & Arts / Alamy Stock Photo.
Illustration by Anne Anderson from The Shoes which were Danced to Pieces
© Look and Learn / Bridgeman Images.

First published in 2021 by Usborne Publishing Ltd.,
Usborne House, 83-85 Saffron Hill, London EC1N 8RT, England.
usborne.com Copyright © 2021 Usborne Publishing Ltd.